Who stole the money?

"Is that the money that disappeared?" Sally asked.

Mr. O'Hara nodded. "When I got back to the store, the lunch rush had started. I put the change in the cash register and placed the three bills in a big envelope on the shelf underneath the counter. When I looked for it after lunch, it had disappeared."

"Did you ask your employees about it?" Encyclopedia asked.

"Yes, I told them there was money missing. They all said they hadn't seen it," Mr. O'Hara said, "but they were the only ones behind the counter. I looked everywhere. The envelope didn't walk off the shelf. It's gone!"

Read all the books in the Encyclopedia Brown series!

Encyclopedia Brown Boy Detective

*Encyclopedia Brown and the
Case of the Secret Pitch*

Encyclopedia Brown Finds the Clues

Encyclopedia Brown Gets His Man

Encyclopedia Brown Solves Them All

Encyclopedia Brown Keeps the Peace

Encyclopedia Brown Saves the Day

Encyclopedia Brown Tracks Them Down

Encyclopedia Brown Shows the Way

Encyclopedia Brown Takes the Case

Encyclopedia Brown Lends a Hand

*Encyclopedia Brown and the
Case of the Dead Eagles*

*Encyclopedia Brown and the
Case of the Midnight Visitor*

Encyclopedia Brown Cracks the Case

Encyclopedia Brown

Super Sleuth

BY DONALD J. SOBOL

illustrated by James Bernardin

PUFFIN BOOKS
An Imprint of Penguin Group (USA) Inc.

PUFFIN BOOKS

Published by the Penguin Group

Penguin Young Readers Group, 345 Hudson Street, New York, New York 10014, U.S.A.
Penguin Group (Canada), 90 Eglinton Avenue East, Suite 700,
Toronto, Ontario, Canada M4P 2Y3 (a division of Pearson Penguin Canada Inc.)
Penguin Books Ltd, 80 Strand, London WC2R 0RL, England
Penguin Ireland, 25 St Stephen's Green, Dublin 2, Ireland (a division of Penguin Books Ltd)
Penguin Group (Australia), 250 Camberwell Road, Camberwell, Victoria 3124, Australia
(a division of Pearson Australia Group Pty Ltd)
Penguin Books India Pvt Ltd, 11 Community Centre,
Panchsheel Park, New Delhi - 110 017, India
Penguin Group (NZ), 67 Apollo Drive, Rosedale, North Shore 0632, New Zealand
(a division of Pearson New Zealand Ltd.)
Penguin Books (South Africa) (Pty) Ltd, 24 Sturdee Avenue,
Rosebank, Johannesburg 2196, South Africa

Registered Offices: Penguin Books Ltd, 80 Strand, London WC2R 0RL, England

First published in the United States of America by Dutton Children's Books,
a division of Penguin Young Readers Group, 2009
Published by Puffin Books, a division of Penguin Young Readers Group, 2010

3 5 7 9 10 8 6 4 2

LIBRARY OF CONGRESS CATALOGING-IN-PUBLICATION DATA IS AVAILABLE
ISBN: 978-0-525-42100-9 (hc)

Puffin Books ISBN 978-0-14- 241688-4

Printed in the United States of America

Design by Jason Henry
Text set in Janson

For Dennis Wepman and Warren Wightman

Before Time Runs Out

CONTENTS

1   The Case of the Hollow Tree   1

2   The Case of the Headless Ghost   10

3   The Case of the Stolen Moonstone   19

4   The Case of the Disappearing Hundreds   27

5   The Case of the Patriotic Volunteer   34

6   The Case of the Stolen Watch   41

7   The Case of the Gym Bag   49

8   The Case of the Supercomputer Brain   56

9   The Case of the Giggling Goldilocks   63

10   The Case of Shoeless Sam   71

   Solutions   78

The Case of the Hollow Tree

In every city and town across the United States, crime was a serious problem. Except in Idaville. For more than a year no one, grown-up or child, had gotten away with breaking the law there.

Apart from winning its war on crime, Idaville was like most other seaside towns. It had beautiful white beaches and lovely parks, churches and a synagogue, and banks and delicatessens. On rainy summer afternoons, the movie theaters played double features.

Police chiefs from Maine to California scratched their heads in wonder at Idaville's success in catching criminals. They decided that Idaville's police chief, Chief Brown, was a genius.

Chief Brown was indeed both smart and brave. However the real genius behind the town's perfect arrest record was his ten-year-old son, Encyclopedia. Whenever Chief Brown had a crime he could not solve, he knew what to do. He cleaned off his desk, put on his hat, and went home to dinner. Encyclopedia solved the crime at the table. Usually, he needed to ask just one question.

Chief Brown wanted to see Encyclopedia's picture hanging in the National Detective Hall of Fame. However, he couldn't tell a soul. Who would believe that the mastermind behind the crime cleanup was his only child, Encyclopedia? So he said nothing.

Encyclopedia never told anyone about the help he gave his father. He didn't want to seem different from other fifth graders.

There was nothing he could do about his nickname. Only his parents and teachers called him by his real name, Leroy. Everyone else called him Encyclopedia. An encyclopedia is a book or set of books filled with facts from *A* to *Z*. So was Encyclopedia's head. He never forgot anything he read. His friends joked that he was better than a computer for looking up answers to their questions. He never crashed!

Monday evening Chief Brown came home from work in a happy mood. He complimented Mrs. Brown on the mushroom soup, and asked for seconds of the roast beef.

"Did anything exciting happen at work today?" Mrs. Brown asked.

"Indeed it did," said Chief Brown. "We caught one of the two bank robbers who have been hitting banks all over the state. He was running from the Idaville National Bank when he tripped and fell. His partner took off in the getaway car without him."

Encyclopedia looked up from his mashed potatoes. Crime always grabbed his attention.

"I read about those men in this morning's

newspaper," Mrs. Brown said. "They wore masks and used a different stolen getaway car for every robbery."

Chief Brown nodded. "That's them," he said.

"Is the other robber still on the loose?" Mrs. Brown asked.

"Yes, but we'll catch him soon enough," Chief Brown told her.

Encyclopedia was surprised by his father's cheerfulness. "Did the man you arrested give you the other bank robber's name?" Encyclopedia asked.

"No, he's too frightened of his partner. He did tell us where the money is hidden," Chief Brown said. "It's hidden in the state park, in a hollowed-out sycamore tree. Officer McDonald is staking out the spot. I'm going to join him after dinner."

"Can I go with you, Dad?" Encyclopedia asked. Catching criminals was one of his favorite things to do.

"Sure, you can."

Encyclopedia let out a whoop. Just being together with his father was a huge thrill.

"Are you sure there won't be any danger?" Mrs. Brown asked.

"The robbers used toy guns to commit their crimes," Chief Brown assured her. "Leroy will be perfectly safe. As soon as the man finds the tree and retrieves the money, we'll arrest him."

After dinner, Chief Brown and Encyclopedia drove to the state park outside of town. Encyclopedia had gone camping and fishing there with his friends many times.

Officer McDonald jumped to his feet as they drew near. A flashlight wobbled in his shaking hand. "Arrest! You're under . . . Stop!" he yelled.

"It's only me, officer," Chief Brown said calmly. "He just graduated from the Police Academy," he whispered to Encyclopedia. "This is his first stakeout."

"Sorry, Chief." The embarrassed officer crouched behind a giant rock.

Chief Brown and Encyclopedia settled behind

a bush. It was so dark, Encyclopedia wondered how the robber would ever find the right tree.

The officer trained his eyes on the forest. "Stop, you're under arrest," he whispered to himself. "Stop, you're under arrest."

It was a cloudy night. No stars were visible. The moon played hide-and-seek. Encyclopedia and the two men waited quietly, straining their eyes against the darkness. Officer McDonald jumped at every sound. An owl's hoot made him gasp. A rabbit's hop sent him leaping.

Finally, they heard a faint tapping. It grew closer and closer to where the officers and Encyclopedia were staked out. The tapping continued from tree to tree.

A man with a walking stick stopped in front of one tree. He counted to himself as he tapped the stick against the tree trunk.

Encyclopedia saw Officer McDonald stiffen. Before Encyclopedia or Chief Brown could stop him, the officer jumped to his feet and shouted, "Stop. You're under arrest!"

He had gotten the words right, but the officer dropped his flashlight nervously. Chief Brown stepped forward and picked up the light.

The suspect raised his arms. His walking stick dropped from his hands. "Under arrest?" he said, blinking in the harsh glow of the flashlight. "For taking a walk in these lovely woods?"

"You're the bank robber. You were getting ready to get the money that you and your partner hid in the tree," Officer McDonald said. "He told us all about it! It's inside a hollowed out tree."

"Tree? How on earth would I find the right tree in the pitch-black?" the man asked. "I don't have a map. I don't have a flashlight. I was simply taking a walk on a cloudy night. You can't prove that I've done anything wrong."

Officer McDonald searched the man and didn't find a map or a flashlight. It was only then he realized his mistake. He should have waited for the man to uncover the stolen money before he tried to make an arrest.

"Stop. You're under arrest!"

"I've ruined everything, haven't I?" he said quietly to Chief Brown. "We have no proof he's the bank robber."

Chief Brown looked from the thief to Officer McDonald and back again. Idaville's perfect arrest record was in danger.

"Without a map, we have no evidence that the man was looking for the money hidden in the hollow tree," the Chief said quietly. "I don't think there's anything we can do unless we get his partner to identify him. By then this man will have left the state."

"He may not have had a map, but he definitely knew how to find the right tree," Encyclopedia said.

HOW WAS ENCYCLOPEDIA ABLE TO PROVE THAT THE MAN WAS THE BANK ROBBER?

(Turn to page 78 for the solution to "The Case of the Hollow Tree.")

The Case of the Headless Ghost

In the winter Encyclopedia did his detective work in the dining room. That and schoolwork kept him busy. When school let out for the summer, he set up his own detective agency in the garage. He shared his office with his father's car. As soon as Chief Brown left for work in the mornings, Encyclopedia opened for business.

Every summer morning he hung his sign outside the garage:

BROWN DETECTIVE AGENCY
13 Rover Avenue
Leroy Brown, President
No case too small
25¢ per day
plus expenses

He sat at a battered old desk next to a red gasoline can and waited for customers.

One morning, he watched the children of the neighborhood run past his driveway. Not one of them stopped. Finally Davy Jones slowed down long enough to let Encyclopedia know what was happening.

Idaville, being a seaside town, had its share of pirate history. Davy Jones was crazy about pirates. Today he wore a black eye patch and a red bandanna tied around his head. He waved a small pirate flag.

"Ahoy, matey," he yelled. "Ye best set sail, or it's a ghostly treasure you'll be missin' out on."

"Shiver me timbers!" Encyclopedia said, playing along. "Who's the ghost and where's the treasure?"

"It's Old Cutthroat Flint. He's haunting Idaville," Davy explained.

Encyclopedia had heard of Old Cutthroat Flint—everyone in Idaville had. The pirate hid out in the area back in the 1800s when his ship,

The Scurvy Serpent, needed repairs. Legend had it that Old Cutthroat buried his pirate's booty before setting sail.

Old Cutthroat was famously mean, even for a pirate. His buccaneers staged a mutiny, and Old Cutthroat lost his head. His body was said to be sailing the Seven Seas, searching for his head. His treasure had never been found.

"Bugs Meany is selling peeks at the ghost for ten cents," Davy said. "For a quarter you can talk to the ghost. That's why I'm dressed like this. I'm going to ask him where he buried his gold doubloons. If he thinks I'm a pirate, he might tell!"

"Bugs Meany?" Encyclopedia asked.

Davy nodded. "Old Cutthroat is haunting the Tigers' clubhouse. Bugs said he showed up just last night."

Encyclopedia immediately knew something was wrong. Bugs was the leader of a gang of tough older boys. They called themselves the Tigers. They should have called themselves the

Pirates. They "sailed the seas" of Idaville, always ready to steal the treasure of the small kids. Encyclopedia would have liked to make all the Tigers walk the plank.

"*Arrrrrgh*," Davy continued, "Bugs knows it's Old Cutthroat because it's a headless ghost."

"How will the ghost tell you where to find the treasure if it doesn't have a mouth?" Encyclopedia asked.

Davy lowered his pirate flag, the Jolly Roger. "You don't believe Bugs?"

"I'd sooner believe cats bark," Encyclopedia told him.

"I don't want to miss out on seeing a real pirate ghost, if there is one," Davy said. He plunked a quarter on the gas can beside Encyclopedia. "I'm hiring you. Come with me and prove the ghost is a fake." He pulled a candy bar from his pocket. "This will help you think better."

"I'm sure of it," the boy detective said. He accepted the candy before Davy changed his mind.

Together, the boys set off for the Tigers'

clubhouse, an unused toolshed behind Mr. Sweeney's Auto Body Shop. Strange sounds started to come toward them when they were about a block away. The closer they got, the more eerie the sounds became. There were screeches and moans, and one very loud *"Aaarrrggghh!"*

Suddenly, Melissa Chambers raced past, holding her ears. "A ghost! A ghost!" she screamed.

A line of kids had nervously formed outside the Tigers' clubhouse. Bugs and Duke Kelly, a Tiger, stood in front of the closed door. A black curtain hung over the window. As kids deposited their dimes in Bugs's hand, Duke Kelly pulled back the curtain and let them peek inside. An orange crate was nearby for the shorter kids.

Encyclopedia and Davy took their places at the end of the line.

"Step up and pay your dime to see the headless ghost," Bugs said. "Remember, it's a dime to peek in the window and a quarter to enter the pirate's cabin. Ask him where he hid his pirate's booty—if you dare."

Encyclopedia's friend Fangs Liverright was at the front of the line. He handed a dime to Bugs and stepped up to the window.

"Remember, he doesn't have a head," Bugs said. "He's wearing one of our Tiger T-shirts, so you'll be able to see his invisible ghost's body."

Fangs nodded and Duke Kelly pulled back the curtain.

At that moment there was a loud, angry howl from inside the shed. Fangs shook as if he'd just been dipped in electricity.

The kids on line behind him wanted to know what Fangs saw.

"It's a headless ghost all right," Fangs said, "and boy is he mad! I wouldn't go inside if I were you."

Davy swallowed. "Maybe going in to see Old Cutthroat isn't such a good idea. I think I'll just peek in the window. He might think I'm one of the pirates that cut off his head."

"Yo-ho-ho! You don't have to go inside," Bugs reminded everyone. "For just one thin dime you can peek in the window." He scanned the line and spotted Encyclopedia. "What are you doing here?"

"I'm here to put a stop to your piracy," Encyclopedia told him. "I don't think there's a ghost at all."

"Oh, yeah? Are you brave enough to go inside and face this ghost you don't believe in?" Bugs asked with a sneer. "Or are you too chicken-hearted?"

There was a low growl from inside the shed, followed by a loud roar. "Fetch my cat-o'-nine-tails. I've a couple of landlubbers to be teachin' a lesson."

"I-it's the ghost," Davy stammered.

He slipped his quarter into Encyclopedia's hand. "You go ahead. I don't need any pirate's booty," he said. His teeth were chattering.

Suddenly, Encyclopedia didn't think facing the headless ghost was such a good idea, either.

Bugs smirked at him, and Duke Kelly let out a loud snicker. Encyclopedia handed over the quarter.

"Remember, we're not responsible for what happens in there. It was your idea to face the ghost," Bugs said to Encyclopedia.

"I think I'll make a daring escape," Davy said.

Bugs turned to Duke. "On the count of three."

"One. Two. Three!" they said together. Duke opened the door, and Bugs pushed Encyclopedia inside. The door closed behind him with a slam.

Encyclopedia found himself face-to-chest with a white Tigers T-shirt in the dark shed. Whatever wore it definitely did not have a head.

"Landlubber!" the T-shirt screamed. "Scalawag! Is it me treasure ye be after?"

Encyclopedia cleared his throat. "Is there a treasure?" he asked.

"Not for a sprog like you!" the T-shirt said.

Encyclopedia's eyes darted around the shed. A fly settled on Encyclopedia's forehead. He chased it away with a clenched hand.

"What's that ye be hiding in your hand?" Old Cutthroat demanded. "A trick?"

"No. It's a candy bar," Encyclopedia told him.

"I'll have that!" the headless creature yelled, grabbing the candy bar. "Be gone with you."

The ghost dropped behind a pile of orange crates, the door opened, and Encyclopedia felt himself being pulled outside.

"I told you it was a real ghost," Bugs said triumphantly. "And you can't prove otherwise."

Encyclopedia held out his hand, palm up. "Give me back my quarter, Bugs. And give everyone back their dimes. That's no ghost."

HOW DID ENCYCLOPEDIA KNOW?

(Turn to page 79 for the solution to "The Case of the Headless Ghost.")

The Case of the
Stolen Moonstone

Bugs Meany had one overwhelming wish. It was to get back at Encyclopedia. He longed to punch the boy detective so hard on the jaw he'd have to laugh through his nose.

Even so, as much as Bugs hated being out-smarted over and over again, he never raised a fist. Every time he felt like it, his own teeth started to hurt. That's because he remembered Encyclopedia's junior partner, Sally Kimball.

Sally was a triple threat. She was the best ath-lete and the prettiest girl in the fifth grade. She was also one of the nicest. She hated bullies and always stood up for the underdog.

The first time Sally saw Bugs, he was bullying a Cub Scout. She jumped off her bike and shouted, "Stop it!"

"Scram, kiddie, or I'll put you facedown on your back," Bugs growled.

Sally did not waste time talking. She stepped in and boxed his ears with lefts and rights, *rap-tap-tap*. Then her right went into his belly, *whammo*!

Bugs staggered around like a boy hunting a stomach pump.

Because of Sally, Bugs never bullied Encyclopedia. However, Bugs didn't stop trying to get revenge. He only gave up the idea of using force.

"Bugs won't stop until he gets back at you," Sally warned one morning while they were opening the detective agency. "He's trouble."

"Bugs hates you as much as he hates me," Encyclopedia said. "He'll get even any way he can."

"Let him try."

"Bugs was watching me when I left Rico Ayres's house last night," Encyclopedia said.

"The new boy? He lives right next door to Bugs, right?" Sally said.

Encyclopedia nodded. Rico had moved to Idaville from Glenn City just a few weeks before. "He invited me over to see his insect collection." Encyclopedia said. "The whole time I was at his house he kept looking out the window at Bugs's house. He seemed scared.

"I asked him about Bugs. He told me he hadn't met his neighbors yet," Encyclopedia continued.

"Did you see his insect collection?" Sally asked.

"He was more interested in showing me his grandmother's moonstone ring than his scorpions. He kept looking over my shoulder and out the window. I left before he brought out his centipede collection."

Just then a police car pulled into Encyclopedia's driveway. Officer Lopez was behind the wheel. Bugs Meany and Rico Ayres sat in the backseat. They all got out of the car.

"There he is, officer!" Bugs said. "He's the one I saw leaving Rico's house last night."

"Is that right, Encyclopedia? Were you at Rico's house last night?" Officer Lopez asked.

"I was. And Bugs watched me leave," Encyclopedia said calmly. "I went over to see Rico's insect collection. Right, Rico?"

Rico shuffled his foot on the driveway. "I wasn't home last night," he mumbled. "I was in Glenn City with my family."

Officer Lopez had opened his mouth to ask another question when Bugs broke in.

"I saw a light, like a flashlight, bouncing from room to room in Rico's house last night," Bugs said. "Rico had told me earlier that he was going to Glenn City with his family, so I thought the light was suspicious. I watched the house. I saw someone climb out of a window onto the back porch, as bold as you please. I got a good look at his face, too. It was Encyclopedia Brown!"

"There he is, officer! He's the one I saw leaving
Rico's house last night."

"Of course he was as bold as you please," Sally said. "Encyclopedia has nothing to hide."

"And I left by the door, not the window," Encyclopedia added.

"There's an expensive ring missing from the Ayres's house," Officer Lopez told them. "Someone stole it while the family was out last night."

"Rico was home! Encyclopedia said so," Sally insisted.

Rico's eyes darted nervously from Sally's clenched fist to Bugs's narrowed eyes. "I was in Glenn City," he said again.

"If Encyclopedia was seen leaving the house when the family was away from home, I'm afraid that makes him a suspect," Officer Lopez told Sally.

"More than a suspect," Bugs said. "He's a thief. Robbing one house wasn't enough for him. He came over to mine and put his hands right up against the window to peer inside." Bugs held his hands up and put his face between them to demonstrate. "He had a ring on his finger, and I saw the stone. It was round and white, like the moon.

"I was too frightened to show myself," Bugs continued. "He's a dangerous character and I was home alone. So I turned on a couple of lights and made lots of noise to scare him away. He ran off down the street."

"One more lie like that and you won't be able to run faster than a duck, Bugs Meany!" Sally said.

"The idol of America's youth doesn't lie, and I'm the idol," Bugs bellowed. "You'd better question her, too," Bugs told Officer Lopez, pointing at Sally. "She's his criminal sidekick. He's the brain and she's the brawn. Everyone is too frightened of them to come forward, but I'll be the town's hero if I have to be."

"Do something, Encyclopedia!" Sally said.

Officer Lopez tried to calm the situation. "Encyclopedia, I think we'd better go to the station and discuss this with your father. You admit to being at the house, an expensive piece

of jewelry is missing, and we have a witness"—
she glanced at Bugs—"who claims to have seen
you wearing the ring."

"We can go see my father if you'd like," Encyclopedia said, "but Bugs is lying about the
ring."

HOW DID ENCYCLOPEDIA KNOW?

(Turn to page 80 for the solution to "The Case of the
Stolen Moonstone.")

The Case of the
Disappearing Hundreds

Encyclopedia and Sally decided to celebrate solving their latest case with a special afternoon treat. That meant Mr. O'Hara's drugstore and old-fashioned soda fountain. He made the biggest and best chocolate ice-cream sodas in Idaville.

They took the number five bus downtown and got off in front of the First National Bank on Beach Street. They met Mr. O'Hara coming out of his drugstore. He was wringing his hands.

"Leroy, I was just on my way to see your father," Mr. O'Hara said.

"He's in Glenn City this afternoon," Encyclopedia told him. "They asked him to help on a case there."

"I guess my problem can wait until he returns," Mr. O'Hara said with a heavy sigh.

"Is something wrong?" Sally said.

"One of my employees is a thief," Mr. O'Hara said unhappily. "I can't believe one of them would steal from me. It's not merchandise that's missing. It's money. Three one-hundred-dollar bills."

Sally gasped. "That sure would buy a lot of ice cream."

"I'll tell my father to call you when he gets home," Encyclopedia promised. He wanted to try and solve the crime himself but didn't want to boast. "Can you tell us the details?"

"I've had a very good month," Mr. O'Hara told the young detectives. "This hot weather is great for the soda fountain trade, and the drugstore side of my business has been booming, too."

"An ice-cream soda on a hot day sure does hit the spot," Sally agreed.

Mr. O'Hara nodded. "I hired a new employee, Wendy Schraft, a few weeks ago to help keep up with the demand. Wendy changed some of our displays. Her new toothpaste display sent sales soaring. They're up fifty percent."

"Wow, that's a lot of clean teeth," Sally said.

"Wendy works mostly in the drugstore. She only fills in at the soda fountain when we're busy," Mr. O'Hara explained. "My other two employees, George Meade and Bob Sherman, have been with me for years. Bob mans the fountain and George mostly takes orders, but everyone pitches in when we're busy and does whatever needs to be done."

Encyclopedia had been at the busy soda fountain many times. He knew both George and Bob.

"I wanted to thank them all for their hard work," said Mr. O'Hara. "When I went to the bank this morning to get change for the cash register, I also got three crisp one-hundred-dollar bills to give to them as a bonus. I was going to surprise them this afternoon."

"Is that the money that disappeared?" Sally asked.

Mr. O'Hara nodded. "When I got back to the store, the lunch rush had started. I put the change in the cash register and placed the three bills in a big envelope on the shelf underneath the counter. When I looked for it after lunch, it had disappeared."

"Did you ask your employees about it?" Encyclopedia asked.

"Yes, I told them there was money missing. They all said they hadn't seen it," Mr. O'Hara said, "but they were the only ones behind the counter. I looked everywhere. The envelope didn't walk off the shelf. It's gone!"

Mr. O'Hara opened the door and ushered the two detectives inside the store.

It was mid-afternoon and there were few customers. George was filling the napkin holders. Encyclopedia could see Bob washing dishes in the back room. Wendy was on the other side of the store, creating a new shampoo display.

Mr. O'Hara tried to be hopeful. "Encyclopedia will speak to his father tonight about the theft," he said to George. "The thief will be caught in no time."

Encyclopedia and Sally took stools at the fountain near the cash register. There was no need to look at the menu. They both wanted chocolate ice-cream sodas.

"Did any customers go behind the counter during the lunch rush?" Encyclopedia asked George.

"Not that I saw," George answered. "I did leave once to get more hot dog and hamburger rolls, so I can't be absolutely positive."

He began spooning ice cream into two glasses. "Wendy went back and forth a few times," he continued. "She filled in when I was gone, and came back again later when we were busy. I hate to call her a thief, but Bob and I have worked for Mr. O'Hara for years. Wendy has only worked here a few weeks."

"It wasn't me," Wendy said, coming up behind them. "I helped out at the counter when I was needed. I didn't see any bank envelope. It must have been George or Bob." She stamped her foot. "Someone's trying to pin this on me because I'm new."

"It sure wasn't me," George said. "I didn't touch Mr. O'Hara's Ben Franklins. It had to have been Bob. He moves back and forth between the counter and the kitchen all the time."

He didn't see that Bob was right behind him with a tray of clean glasses.

"I'm no thief." Bob put the tray down and stormed off. Then he marched back. "If anyone here thinks I'm a thief, I'll leave right now. I can get another job."

"Everyone, let's get back to work," Mr. O'Hara said anxiously. "We can't solve this now. Leroy will discuss it with his father and then we'll see what's what."

George put the chocolate ice-cream sodas in front of the two detectives.

Encyclopedia closed his eyes. He always

closed his eyes when he did his deepest thinking. Then he quietly asked Mr. O'Hara one question. "Did you tell anyone what was in the bank envelope?"

"No, I didn't. I can't afford to give them a bonus if the money isn't returned. I didn't want to get their hopes up."

Sally took a sip of her soda. "It must have been Wendy," she said to Encyclopedia. "Check the shampoo display. The envelope is probably hidden behind one of the bottles."

Encyclopedia shook his head.

"George and Bob have worked for Mr. O'Hara for such a long time. They wouldn't steal from him," Sally said.

"One of them did," Encyclopedia said. "It was . . ."

WHO WAS THE THIEF?

(Turn to page 81 for the solution to "The Case of the Disappearing Hundreds.")

The Case of the
Patriotic Volunteer

Business was slow Wednesday afternoon, so Encyclopedia and Sally walked to the park. They heard that local magician Donald Martinez was going to try out his new act and not charge. Instead of finding a man in a magician's hat they found one wearing a white top hat with blue stripes and white stars.

The man stood in front of the gazebo at the center of the park. A small group of children had gathered around him. As Encyclopedia drew closer, he noticed that the man was dressed in a blue jacket, a white shirt, a red bow tie, and red-and-white striped pants. He held a United States flag and waved it as he talked.

Mary Lukeman greeted the detectives excitedly. "Encyclopedia! Sally! Wait until you hear about this new charity. It's a wonderful thing for the children of America."

She turned to the man. "Start from the beginning again, Mr. Jefferson," she urged. "Encyclopedia and Sally will want to help."

"Happy to, young lady," Mr. Jefferson said, tipping his hat. His gaze swept over the children. "I've left my home in Washington, D.C., our nation's capital, to travel across the country. The president of the United States has asked me spread the word about a wonderful new opportunity for the children of America."

"The president of the United States!" Mary shouted, her eyes bright with excitement. "Imagine that!"

Mr. Jefferson nodded. "The president of the United States."

"Get to the point," Bugs Meany demanded. "What's so wonderful?"

"It's the chance of a lifetime," Mr. Jefferson told him. "Our new charity, Washington Wishes, will search for the children of America with the best ideas for our country. Then we'll take the children to Washington, D.C."

Mary turned to Encyclopedia. "Washington, D.C.!" she shouted.

"Washington, D.C." Mr. Jefferson repeated. "There, they'll get to share their thoughts with the president. Your ideas will make this great country even greater."

The children gasped.

"As soon as I heard about this idea, I told the president to sign me up as his first volunteer," Mr. Jefferson said. "I want to help children share their hopes and dreams for the country with the president of the United States. I'll bet you all have good ideas."

"Abolish school!" Bugs Meany shouted.

The Tigers cheered his idea.

"No more baths!" Rocky Graham, a Tiger, said.

"A swimming pool in every backyard!" Bugs added.

The Tigers applauded, but the rest of the children were more serious.

"Bullies would be thrown in jail," Mary Lukeman said, glaring at Bugs.

"Better pay for schoolteachers," Sally added.

Bugs drowned her out with boos, but Sally shouted him down.

"A great education for all!" she said. She raised her fist and whispered so only Bugs and Encyclopedia could hear. *"Pow!"*

Bugs quieted down pretty quick at the sight of Sally's fist. Mr. Jefferson continued with his talk.

"All those great ideas are going to cost money," he said. "That's the other part of my job. The president asked me to collect money from the children of America. It's only fitting that the children will be the ones to pay for this fantastic new charity."

The man looked around. "Who wants to help the children of America change the world?"

Mary Lukeman raised her hand. "I do."

The other children followed her lead.

"Let's go to the television station," Mary suggested. "They can do a story, and everyone will be able to donate money."

Mr. Jefferson shook his head. "No. This news is only for children. Let's not get the grown-ups involved." He took off his top hat with a flourish and held it in front of him. "The president and I pledge to help you change the world."

"Do you really know the president?" Sally asked.

"I certainly do," Mr. Jefferson said. He quickly pulled a photograph out of his pocket and held it up in the air for everyone to see. It was a picture of himself and the president, standing in front of the Washington Monument.

"I visit him and his family all the time at their home in the Capitol building," Mr. Jefferson told Sally. "And I can't wait to tell him about you

"The president and I pledge to help you change the world."

and the other children of this fine town. All it will take is a generous donation from each of you."

Mary Lukeman was the first to reach into her pocket. She dropped a quarter into the hat. "Don't leave town yet," she urged Mr. Jefferson. "I have to run home and get my piggy bank!"

"Save your money," Encyclopedia told her. He raised his voice so all the children could hear. "Mr. Jefferson might be from Washington, D.C., but he's never visited the president. He's lying."

HOW DID ENCYCLOPEDIA KNOW THAT MR. JEFFERSON WAS LYING?

(Turn to page 82 for the solution to "The Case of the Patriotic Volunteer.")

The Case of the Stolen Watch

One sunny morning, Sally dragged Encyclopedia to the high school to see the Idaville Art Show. Encyclopedia would have rather gone fishing, or to the beach. Sally, however, never missed a chance to see a Pablo Pizarro painting.

Pablo Pizarro was Idaville's greatest boy artist. He had won the Idaville Art Show so often that the town was forced to drop the children's division. No one under twelve dared enter a painting against him. He put his newest work on view, even though he couldn't win a prize.

"Winning prizes isn't important," he had announced. "It would be a crime to deprive the people of an original Pizarro."

"Or bizarro," Encyclopedia had muttered under his breath.

Encyclopedia didn't think very highly of Pablo's art. He didn't see a difference between Pablo's sculptures and junk of the week. Pablo's modern art paintings were another matter. They could have been called magnificent— if you'd handed a paintbrush to a monkey and asked him to make a mess.

Pablo's painting was on display by itself in the lobby.

"It's only fitting," Sally said. "Pablo is in a class by himself."

Encyclopedia only nodded. He didn't dare share his real opinion with Sally. She thought Pablo was an artist of the highest order.

A small crowd had gathered around Pablo and his easel. On it was a painting of a pocket watch with Idaville's City Hall and clock tower in the background. The watch was giant-sized. It seemed to be melting around the edges.

A real pocket watch sat on a table next to the easel.

Sally looked from one to the other. The two didn't look anything alike.

"It's a modern, abstract painting," Pablo explained.

"Ah," Sally nodded wisely.

Punctual Pete Leonard, the human sundial, asked, "What's with the clocks?"

Punctual Pete prided himself on being precisely on time—never late and never early. "Who wants worms?" he was known to ask. "I'm no early bird."

"I call it *Pieces of Time*," Pablo said dramatically. "It's my watch, with Idaville in the background. Hundreds of years from now, when future generations see my painting, they'll have no doubt about my artistic roots in Idaville."

Sally's hand fluttered to her mouth. She often became fluttery when Pablo was around. "Another masterpiece," she said breathlessly.

Pablo beamed at her. He held a painter's palette and brush in one hand. He wiped his brow dramatically with the other. "It's my best work so far."

"I can see that," Sally agreed.

Pablo led the small crowd toward the gym. "Now I must go and encourage my fellow artists. The prizes will be given out soon."

Punctual Pete lagged behind. He didn't want to be early.

Encyclopedia and Sally watched the winners accept their blue ribbons. The detectives were on their way out of the school when they heard Pablo calling their names.

"My pocket watch," he exclaimed. "It's been stolen!"

"Oh no," Sally cried. "The one you used as a model in your masterpiece?"

"Yes, and I think I know who took it," Pablo said. "Punctual Pete Leonard."

"Why Punctual Pete?" Encyclopedia asked.

"He tried to buy my painting for fifty cents," Pablo said angrily. "I told him he was no art lover if he thought my masterpiece wasn't worth at least ten dollars. He got mad and threatened to stop my clock."

Sally shook her head. "That watch will be priceless one day, along with your painting. Encyclopedia, we have to help Pablo get his watch back."

Pablo fished in his pocket for a quarter. "I'm hiring you to catch that crook," he said.

Encyclopedia examined the painting and the area around it for clues. The numbers on the pocket watch in the painting were warped, but he could see that time had stopped at 12:05. He stepped closer to make out the tiny Roman numerals on the painting of the City Hall clock. It was fifteen minutes behind the time of the painted watch.

"Hurry, Encyclopedia," Sally urged. "Let's go talk to Punctual Pete."

They found Pete on his front porch reading a book.

Pablo marched up the front walk and accused him. "You stole my watch, didn't you?"

"Why would I want your old watch?" Pete asked.

"You were looking at my painting while the rest of us went to see who won the art show," Pablo said.

"Anybody could have taken your old watch," Pete responded. "You can't prove it was me." He stood. "Now if you'll excuse me, I can't be late for lunch." He went inside and closed the door behind him.

Pablo kicked a porch step. "I know he has my watch."

Sally seemed uncertain. She glanced nervously at Encyclopedia.

Encyclopedia was uncertain, too.

Pablo shook his head sadly. "Artists who are ahead of their times are always treated badly," he said.

They passed City Hall on their way back to the high school.

"At least that clock still stands as a monument to your masterpiece," Sally said.

Encyclopedia looked at the clock. Then he stopped and closed his eyes.

"He's thinking," Sally whispered to Pablo.

"I have a plan to catch whoever took your watch," Encyclopedia said.

"What can I do to help?" Sally asked.

"Spread the word that Pablo will hold an art viewing in the park at four o'clock today." Encyclopedia said. "Tell them not to come before four o'clock, or he won't be ready."

"A viewing?" Pablo asked.

Encyclopedia nodded. "The thief will give himself away," Encyclopedia told him. "I'm sure of it."

"If there is to be a viewing I must create a new masterpiece!" Pablo said, running off.

Encyclopedia and Sally invited everyone they saw to the art viewing.

At 3:30, they went to the park. Pablo placed a sheet over his new painting, ready for the grand unveiling. His white artist's smock was covered in paint.

"What do we do now, Encyclopedia?" Sally asked.

"We just wait," he replied.

"Are you sure you know what you're doing?" she asked.

"We just wait," Encyclopedia said again.

Fifteen minutes later, Punctual Pete arrived. "It's four o'clock, he said. "Where's the big art opening?"

Encyclopedia put out his hand. "First, hand over Pablo's watch," he said.

HOW DID ENCYCLOPEDIA PROVE THAT PUNCTUAL PETE WAS THE THIEF?

(Turn to page 83 for the solution to "The Case of the Stolen Watch.")

The Case of the Gym Bag

Saturday morning, Encyclopedia and his father went to the high school to watch a track meet. Baldy Jones and Fleet Fletcher were running for Idaville. Baldy shaved his head because he thought it made him run faster. Every morning before a big meet he could be found in the barbershop with a head full of shaving cream.

Today's track meet was between Idaville and Glenn City. However, the real contest was between Fleet and Baldy. The runners were both seniors at Idaville High School. They were on the same team, but they were fierce competitors.

They ran in the same races and almost always came in first and second.

Saturday was no different. Encyclopedia and Chief Brown were both on the edge of their seats. Baldy won the 100-meter dash. Fleet edged him out in the 200. Fleet took the hurdles. Baldy ran a faster 400-meter race. In between events, the two runners sneered insults at each other.

The Glenn City team took third place finishes in every single race.

Encyclopedia was hoarse from cheering for Fleet and Baldy by the time the meet was over. He and Chief Brown were weaving through the crowd on their way to the parking lot when they heard shouting from inside the locker room.

Inside, Baldy and Fleet were standing, nose to nose, snarling at each other.

"Hand it over," Fleet yelled, "or you'll wish you never got out of bed this morning."

"I will not! It's mine," Baldy yelled.

"That's my gym bag. Now give it back," Fleet demanded. "Or I'll—"

"You'll what? You try anything and I'll twist your legs so far around your head, you can eat with your feet," Baldy said with a snarl.

"Hah!" Fleet spat. "First a thief and now a bully."

"I am not a thief," Baldy said. "Just because I let you win a couple of races doesn't mean I'll let you have my gym bag, too."

A small crowd had gathered around the two boys. Encyclopedia and Chief Brown pushed their way to the front.

"Chief Brown, arrest him!" Fleet said. "He's stolen my stamp collection."

"I'll stamp you!" Baldy threatened, raising the bag over his head. "It'll be a very rare stamp— one that sends you straight into outer space."

"You just try," Fleet yelled, raising his fists. "You'll be sending me postcards from Jupiter and Mars."

Chief Brown stepped between them. "Boys,

calm down," he said. "Save your competition for the track."

Fleet and Baldy stopped yelling, but they continued to glare at each other.

Chief Brown waited for a moment. "Now, tell me what happened—"

Fleet and Baldy both started to talk at once.

"One at a time, please," Chief Brown said, holding up his hands. "Fleet, you go first."

"Why does he get to go first?" Baldy whined.

"Because he's not holding a gym bag over my head," Chief Brown said calmly.

Baldy sheepishly lowered the bag and handed it to the police chief.

"I showered and changed after the meet," Fleet said, pushing his bangs off his forehead. "I left my gym bag on the bench while I stepped into Coach Lewis's office. When I came out, Baldy was leaving the locker room with *my* gym bag."

"It's *my* gym bag," Baldy insisted. "He's just saying it's his because he knows I have my stamp

"It's my gym bag!"

collection with me today. It's worth a lot of money."

Chief Brown turned to Fleet. "Can you prove this is your gym bag?"

"I mentioned to a couple of guys that I was heading over to the stamp store after the meet to see about selling my collection. There's a collector in town just for today, and he's interested in some of my rare stamps," Fleet explained.

"Is there any identification in the bag?" the chief asked.

Fleet shook his head. "It's a new bag. I didn't think to add an ID tag."

"I was the one who didn't think to add an ID tag," Baldy said. "I can't prove it's mine, either."

The chief opened the bag and pulled out the contents. He lined up the items on the stairs leading to the locker room. Aside from the stamp collection, protected in a plastic folder, the bag held standard items: a damp towel, soap, deodorant, hair gel, and a clean pair of socks.

Fleet checked his wristwatch and moaned.

"The stamp collector is leaving town at five o'clock. It's already four-thirty."

"I'll have to hang on to the gym bag and the stamp collection until I can identify the owner," the chief said. "I'm sorry, but one of you will have to miss the stamp collector."

"Give Fleet his gym bag, Dad," Encyclopedia said. "If he runs like he did at the track meet, he'll get to the stamp store in time."

HOW DID ENCYCLOPEDIA KNOW THE BAG BELONGED TO FLEET?

(Turn to page 84 for the solution to "The Case of the Gym Bag.")

The Case of the
Supercomputer Brain

One sunny morning, Encyclopedia came across Jacob Sampson walking down the street. Jacob seemed to be having a two-sided conversation. He'd ask himself a question, take a swig from a bottle of blue juice, and then answer himself. He was so taken with his own conversation that he banged right into Encyclopedia.

"Who's winning the argument?" Encyclopedia asked.

"I am!" Jacob said excitedly. "I'm going to be the smartest kid in third grade next year. Maybe I'll even skip third grade and go right to college. That's the kind of genius I am."

"How'd you get to be so smart all of a sudden?" Encyclopedia asked.

"With this." Jacob showed Encyclopedia the label on his bottle.

"Supercomputer Brain Liquid," Encyclopedia read. "You drink this and it makes you smart?"

"It makes your brain bigger and better and faster than any computer out there," Jacob explained. "George Perkins invented it. He gave some to Ernie Capra, who didn't know what planet he was from. Now Ernie's as smart as anyone."

George Perkins was a senior at Idaville High School. His grades were so high that teacher's spirits soared when he was in their classes. Not so his best friend, Ernie, whose grades sent them into the depths of despair. Ernie thought the alphabet ended at the letter D, his best grade.

"George sold me a bottle from his small supply," Jacob explained. "Ask me anything."

"What's the capital of Florida?" Encyclopedia asked.

Jacob took a sip of Supercomputer Brain Liquid. "Miami," he said proudly.

"The capital of Florida is Tallahassee," Encyclopedia told him.

Jacob drained his bottle. "Okay, ask me another question."

"Who was the second president of the United States?"

"Thomas Jefferson!"

"No," Encyclopedia said gently. "It was John Adams."

"I guess I didn't drink enough," Jacob said. "I'd better go and buy some more of this stuff. I'll buy every bottle George can spare! I hope Ernie didn't drink it all already."

"You'd be better off investing in some good books," Encyclopedia told him.

"You mean you think Supercomputer Brain Liquid is fake?"

Encyclopedia didn't want to call anyone a liar without proof, so he said nothing.

"I can't believe I let George cheat me," Jacob

groaned. "Here's a quarter. Prove that he's a cheater before he robs anyone else."

"Let's go," Encyclopedia said.

The two boys walked over to Oak Street. George and Ernie stood in George's driveway. A group of younger kids had gathered around them.

"Ernie will demonstrate how my Supercomputer Brain Liquid works," George said. "He drank just two bottles yesterday, and already he's tested at the genius level."

Ernie smiled proudly.

"Ernie, what types of clouds are those?" George asked, pointing to the sky.

"They look like large cotton balls. That makes them cumulus clouds."

"Correct," George said.

The children murmured to each other. Ernie wouldn't have been able to answer that question last week.

The questions got harder and faster, and Ernie answered them all.

"Who discovered the law of gravity?"

"Sir Isaac Newton."

"How many continents are there?"

"Seven."

"Where do polar bears live?"

"The Arctic Circle," Ernie said.

"What year did George Washington become president of the United States?"

"1789."

"What is 11,412 divided by . . ."

"951."

"What year did Columbus discover America?"

"1492."

"What famous document granted the people of the United States life, liberty, and the pursuit of happiness?"

"The Constitution!"

George launched into applause. "Bravo, Ernie! Bravo!"

While the children clapped for Ernie, George got a box from his garage. "I have just a few bottles of this precious liquid left. Those of you who want to be as smart and fast as the world's biggest supercomputer should buy this precious liquid now."

Jacob raised his hand.

"Oh, and here's another satisfied customer," George said, noticing Jacob for the first time. "Jacob bought a bottle just this morning."

"Actually, I uh . . ." Jacob turned to Encyclopedia. "Maybe I just didn't drink enough. Ernie was dumb as a doorknob yesterday and today he knows everything!"

"Jacob, tell me, what's the square root of one hundred," George questioned.

"Twenty-five?" Jacob asked.

"Correct! You see, boys and girls, my Supercomputer Brain Liquid works wonders. Did you know the square root of one hundred when you woke up this morning, Jacob?"

"No," Jacob admitted.

Encyclopedia cleared his throat. "The square root of one hundred is ten, not twenty-five."

George looked confused for a moment. "Jacob, how many bottles of Supercomputer Brain Liquid did you drink?"

"One," Jacob answered.

"Ah! That's the problem. Ernie here drank two bottles. You need another—free of charge." He handed it over. "Okay, kids, two for the price of one. We're having a sale! Get them while you can."

"Save your money," Encyclopedia told them. "Ernie isn't as smart as he thinks he is, and neither is George. They're trying to cheat you."

HOW DID ENCYCLOPEDIA KNOW?

(Turn to page 85 for the solution to "The Case of the Supercomputer Brain.")

The Case of the
Giggling Goldilocks

Sally and Encyclopedia were packing up boxes of some of Encyclopedia's old books to donate to the library.

Sally read the titles. "*Astronomy from A to Z, Dinosaurs*, and *Pyramids*. Didn't you ever read fairy tales when you were little?"

"I was always more interested in science and history," Encyclopedia told her.

Sally was about to tell him how much fun fiction could be when they got a customer.

Patrick Behr marched up Encyclopedia's driveway with an angry scowl. Encyclopedia knew Patrick's soccer team had five wins and zero losses so far this summer. Patrick was known for the Behr Stare. When he was playing goalie, he never got riled. He was impossible to score against. His team depended on him to take them to the state championship.

Today there was no Behr Stare. Patrick's eyes flashed. "That's it! I've had it!" he yelled, slamming a quarter on Encyclopedia's gas can. "You've got to make her stop."

"Make who stop?" Encyclopedia asked.

"Stop what?" Sally said.

"Goldilocks," he spat. "She's been creeping into my house and destroying things when no one's home. I'm sure of it."

Encyclopedia fought to keep a straight face. "The three Behrs are having trouble with Goldilocks?" he asked.

"This is serious," Patrick insisted. "I want you to prove that Goldie Jenkins, my next-door neighbor, has been breaking and entering. I want to have her arrested."

"The five-year-old?" Sally asked. "Mary Jenkins's little sister?"

"That's her," Patrick nodded.

"She's a sweet, little thing," Sally said.

"That sweet, little thing is going to drive me insane," Patrick said through clenched teeth.

"Patrick, you don't need a detective. You need the Brothers Grimm," Sally declared.

Patrick groaned. "You don't understand. She's making my life grim. She's nutty about the story of *Goldilocks and the Three Bears*. Yesterday I came home from soccer practice and found a mess in the kitchen. There was a broken cereal bowl and milk all over the floor. And three boxes of breakfast cereal were completely empty.

"My dad," Patrick continued, "blamed me when he had to go without his crunchy oat flakes this morning. He says I eat like a hungry bear. My mom wasn't too thrilled either. She had to clean up the mess. Goldie playing Goldilocks polished off her wheat squares, along with my granola."

Encyclopedia sympathized. Sometimes his mother accused him of eating like a horse. Even so, he had never eaten three boxes of cereal in one sitting.

"No one believed me when I said that Goldie was the mess maker," Patrick said.

Encyclopedia said, "Did you ask her if she was the one who did all that eating?"

"Yes. She denied it, but she was giggling her head off the whole time. I don't believe her," Patrick replied.

"How did she get in? Were the doors locked?" Encyclopedia asked.

"Our mothers exchanged house keys in case one of us ever gets locked out," Patrick explained. "We used to be good neighbors. Then someone read Goldie that story about the three bears. Now she's sneaking in and eating our cereal!"

"Did she break any chairs?" Sally asked with a laugh.

"No, and she remade my bed. I found a strand of golden hair on my pillow." Patrick held up a strand of long, golden hair as if it were the key piece of evidence in a murder trial.

"That's the color of Goldie's hair all right," Sally said to Encyclopedia. "How can one strand of hair prove that Goldie's been sneaking around in Patrick's house?"

"It can't." Encyclopedia took the evidence from Patrick and studied it for a moment.

"You have to find a way. Please," Patrick pleaded. "If my father has to go another morning without his crunchy oat flakes, I'll be in big trouble."

Encyclopedia, Sally, and Patrick headed over to the Jenkins' house on Worth Street. Mrs. Behr was taking bags of groceries out of her car. The three friends stopped to help. Encyclopedia noticed that the bag he carried contained three different types of breakfast cereal—one for each member of the family. Mrs. Behr was replacing what Goldilocks ate.

They found Goldie Jenkins in her backyard. She had teddy bears lined up—a papa bear, a mama bear, and a small baby bear with a big smile. Goldie pretended to read from a book of fairy tales. Encyclopedia could tell that she was making up the story as she went along.

"The whole wheat squares were too yucky," she said with a giggle. "And the granola was too sweet, but the crunchy oat flakes were just right!"

"Hi, Goldie," Sally said. "Do you know my friend Encyclopedia?"

Goldie giggled in response.

"Hi, Goldie," Encyclopedia said. "Do you see this hair?" He showed her the strand of golden hair.

Goldie giggled some more.

"Patrick said he found it on his pillow. Did you leave it there, or was it the *real* Goldilocks?"

"I am the *real* Goldilocks," she answered. "See my bears? We're friends now."

"So if you're the real Goldilocks, you must have been the one who ate the cereal in Patrick's house and slept in his bed."

"Hi, Goldie. Do you know my friend Encyclopedia?"

"It was you, admit it," Patrick snarled.

"It wasn't me. I wouldn't sleep in his bed," she giggled. "He sleeps on sheets with pictures of superheroes on them."

Patrick stared at the ground; his cheeks blazed. "I have to," he muttered. "My grandmother gave them to me for my birthday."

Encyclopedia turned toward Patrick's backyard. He saw an old swing set and a tree house.

Sally and Patrick followed his gaze.

"I guess that's it," Sally said. "There's no way to prove she was in the house."

Patrick shook his head with a sigh. "I'll have to give up soccer and guard the kitchen or live unhappily ever after."

"Oh, she was in Patrick's house," Encyclopedia said. "And in his bed."

HOW DID ENCYCLOPEDIA KNOW?

(Turn to page 86 for the solution to "The Case of the Giggling Goldilocks.")

The Case of Shoeless Sam

Pinky Plummer, one of Encyclopedia's best pals, dodged a puddle and ran up the Browns' driveway. The sun had just come out after a rainy morning.

"Shoeless Sam is back from the mountains, and he challenged the Idaville Sluggers to a baseball game," he said. "Charlie Stewart's going to save us seats. C'mon!"

Encyclopedia grabbed his hat and glove. Shoeless Sam, of the Idaville Gators, was the town's most entertaining baseball player and now one of the best. He wasn't always a good player. He used to get stuck so far out in the outfield that his glove had never even met a ball.

One day, bored and hot, he took his shoes and socks off and lounged in the grass. He caught a freak fly ball with his toes, and ever since he had been known as Shoeless Sam.

That lucky catch had somehow turned him into a great baseball player. He went back to using his hands, but left his sneakers at home. He even brought his own homemade cloth baseball bases to games so they would not hurt his feet. He pitched fastballs, made double plays, and hit more home runs than anyone in Idaville. All in his bare feet.

This summer, Shoeless Sam had tied the home run record set by Walter Lombardi twenty years before. Mr. Lombardi, who owned the pizza parlor downtown, had promised free pizza for life to the first Idaville player to break his record. Shoeless Sam was just one home run away. Everyone wanted to see him become the new long ball king.

Encyclopedia and Pinky took the number

seven bus to the ball field and chatted excitedly about the game ahead. The Gators had a running rivalry with the Idaville Sluggers. They had played four times this season, and each team had won two games. Today's contest would decide the ultimate winner.

Encyclopedia and Pinky joined their friends Herb Stein and Charlie Stewart in the bleachers. Sally sat two rows behind them with Billy and Jody Turner.

Would Shoeless Sam become the new home run king?

Shoeless Sam struck out three times in the first four innings. Each time, the crowd groaned. They began to wonder, had Shoeless lost his magic? Had his lucky feet been damaged by cold mountain air? Maybe he needed to put his shoes back on.

The teams were tied two to two at the top of the ninth inning. Shoeless Sam was on deck, warming up. Spike Johnson swung and connected with the ball. He made it to first base.

Shoeless Sam took one more practice swing

and then dug his toes into the damp dirt in the batter's box. The crowd quieted. Only the catcher could be heard, making nonsense noises to distract the batter.

Shoeless Sam focused on the ball in the pitcher's hand. Encyclopedia watched the baseball fly through the air. Shoeless Sam's bat came around and connected with the ball with a loud *thwack*!

The crowd was on its feet, and Shoeless Sam was on his way. He was leaving second base. Two more bases to go! An outfielder was chasing the ball. Would Shoeless pass third and get to home base before the ball did?

Suddenly, a member of the Sluggers ran out from the dugout and leaped on the second baseman. The crowd's view of third was blocked as the players moved around each other with their fists raised.

The umpire got the players under control, and Encyclopedia turned back to see Shoeless Sam plant his foot on home base. He had become the new home run king!

The Gators all ran over to congratulate him.

"Wait a minute!" the Sluggers' third baseman said, waving the ball. "Shoeless Sam never came near third. I caught the ball right after the fight broke out. He saw that I was going to tag him out and he ran straight to home. He didn't get a home run. He cheated!"

Pinky turned to Encyclopedia. "That can't be true," he said. "Shoeless Sam wouldn't lie about something like that."

Charlie Stewart shook his head. "His lucky streak is over, and he's trying to cover it up."

"I'll see what's happening," Encyclopedia told them.

He walked over to the umpire, who stood between an angry Shoeless Sam and the Sluggers' third baseman. "I was breaking up the fight," the umpire said. "I couldn't see third base."

"No one could," said one of Sam's teammates. "If you had the ball, why didn't you throw it to home base?" he asked.

"Because he was out at third," the baseman said. "There was no reason to throw the ball home."

"Can I help?" Encyclopedia asked.

"I stepped on third," Shoeless Sam said. "I know I did. Help me prove it."

Encyclopedia looked down at home base. There were a few muddy sneaker prints on the white canvas base, and a bare footprint right in the middle. Then he walked to first with the umpire, Shoeless Sam, and half the players from both teams behind him. He found the same muddy footprints on first and second. Third base, however, while dusty, did not have any prints on it at all.

"See," the third baseman said, "I told you he didn't step on third. If he had come near it, I would have tagged him out. He's no home run king."

The umpire shook his head. "You cheated," he said to Shoeless. "Your team just forfeited the game."

Shoeless Sam's own teammates turned their backs on him and started to walk away.

"Stop! Shoeless Sam got his home run," Encyclopedia told them. "It was the Sluggers who cheated, not Shoeless Sam."

HOW DID ENCYCLOPEDIA KNOW?

(Turn to page 87 for the solution to "The Case of Shoeless Sam.")

Solution to *The Case of the Hollow Tree*

The man suspected of being the second bank robber might not have had a map, but he definitely knew how to find the hollow tree. Encyclopedia noticed that the man had paused while walking and tapped on the surrounding trees with his walking stick. That's how he knew which tree had the money hidden inside. The bank robber knew that hollow trees make a different sound when tapped on the outside.

As soon as Encyclopedia pointed out those facts, Chief Brown had enough evidence to arrest the man. The robber cracked and confessed when Officer McDonald slipped the handcuffs on his wrists.

The bank robber went to jail, and Officer McDonald went back to the Police Academy for a class in how to conduct a stakeout.

Solution to *The Case of the Headless Ghost*

The ghost's hands gave him away.

Bugs had come up with his plan after reading about the mystery of Old Cutthroat Flint's treasure in the local paper. Too lazy to search for the treasure himself, he decided to cheat the children of Idaville out of their hard-earned dimes and quarters.

The ghost of Old Cutthroat Flint was really Rocky Graham, a Tiger, in an extra-large T-shirt. He had pulled his head down under the collar, and relied on the dark shed and the pile of orange crates to hide his legs and his lumpy shape.

Bugs didn't think anyone would be brave enough to enter the shed. He never warned Rocky about his hands. When Rocky grabbed Encyclopedia's candy bar with very real hands, the detective knew the ghost was a fake.

Luckily for Encyclopedia and the rest of the kids, Rocky had a sweet tooth.

Rocky handed over the candy bar, and Bugs gave everyone back their dimes, grumbling the whole time.

Solution to *The Case of the Stolen Moonstone*

As soon as Bugs Meany learned that his new neighbor shared an interest in insects with Encyclopedia Brown, he saw a chance to get even with the boy detective. He pretended to be fascinated by spiders himself to gain Rico's trust. Then he bullied the new boy into helping him with his scheme.

As usual, Bugs couldn't outsmart Encyclopedia. His own words tripped him up. Bugs said that when Encyclopedia put his hands up against the window to peer inside, he saw a ring on his finger and that the stone "was round and white, like the moon."

Had he done what Bugs claimed, Encyclopedia's palms would have been up against the window, not the back of his hands. Bugs wouldn't have seen the ring's stone at all. Rings are worn with the stone on the back of the hand, not on the palm.

Encyclopedia pointed out Bugs's mistake, and Rico admitted that Bugs had bullied him into lying. He had his grandmother's ring in his pocket all along.

To show that there were no hard feelings, Encyclopedia and Sally walked Rico home and spent the morning looking at his insect collection.

Solution to *The Case of the Disappearing Hundreds*

The thief was George. He gave himself away when he said he hadn't seen Mr. O Hara's missing Ben Franklins. Ben Franklin's picture is on the hundred-dollar bill.

Mr. O'Hara had told Encyclopedia that the bonuses were going to be a surprise. He normally came back from the bank with change for the cash register, which would be small bills.

The only way George would have guessed that there were hundred-dollar bills in the bank envelope was if he had seen them.

When told his mistake, George confessed. He thought Mr. O'Hara had forgotten to put the change in the register. When he saw the big bills in the envelope, he decided to pocket them.

Bob and Wendy got their bonuses, and George got a copy of the Help Wanted ads.

Solution to *The Case of the Patriotic Volunteer*

Encyclopedia suspected Mr. Jefferson was lying when he said he didn't want to go to the television station.

Encyclopedia knew the children of America would come up with terrific ideas for improving the country. However, sending one man from town to town wasn't the best way to get the news out about the new charity. Who ever heard of a charity that didn't want television coverage?

As patriotic as Mr. Jefferson looked and sounded, he gave himself away when he said he visited the president and his family at their home in the Capitol building. The president of the United States lives in the White House. The Capitol building is where Congress meets.

As soon as Encyclopedia pointed out his mistake, Mr. Jefferson admitted that he was lying. He had had his picture taken with a cardboard cutout of the president on a trip to Washington, D.C., and tried to use the photograph to make some easy money.

Solution to *The Case of the Stolen Watch*

Punctual Pete gave himself away when he arrived at the park early. Pete was normally so punctual that you could set your watch by him.

When Encyclopedia first noticed two different times in Pablo's painting, he thought the town clock might be slow. When Pablo suggested that he was an artist ahead of his time, Encyclopedia realized that the artist had set his watch fifteen minutes ahead.

With that information, he was able to set a trap for the thief.

Punctual Pete relied on Pablo's stolen watch to tell time and arrived at the viewing fifteen minutes early.

When confronted, Pete admitted he had stolen the watch to get back at Pablo for insulting his love of art. He handed over the watch and went back to being punctual.

Solution to *The Case of the Gym Bag*

Baldy lied about the gym bag and the stamp collection. Neither belonged to him. When he overheard Fleet talking about the stamp collector and the value of the stamps, he looked for an opportunity to grab the bag.

When Fleet stepped into the coach's office, Baldy saw his chance. He hadn't counted on getting caught by Fleet.

The items in the gym bag gave Baldy away. He was well known for his shaved head. Baldy had no use for the hair gel in the gym bag. That proved the bag belonged to Fleet.

Fleet made it to the stamp store just in time.

Solution to *The Case of the Supercomputer Brain*

Ernie's memory was bigger than his brainpower. Still, he made two mistakes. First, he answered one of George's questions before George finished asking it. George asked, "What is 11,412 divided by . . . ?" Ernie answered, "951."

How would Ernie know the answer unless he had memorized the question? He didn't give George a chance to ask him to divide 11,412 by 12. Also, the document that grants life, liberty, and the pursuit of happiness is the Declaration of Independence, not the United States Constitution.

When Encyclopedia pointed out these mistakes, George admitted that he had tried to play a trick on Jacob and the rest of the children. He added blue food coloring to bottles of water and stuck phony labels on them. He was trying to earn some easy money.

George gave Jacob his money back and started looking for a real job.

Solution to *The Case of the Giggling Goldilocks*

Goldie gave herself away when she said, "He sleeps on sheets with pictures of superheroes on them." When Encyclopedia saw Patrick's backyard, he knew that Goldie Jenkins had to be the mysterious, cereal-eating visitor.

Encyclopedia saw a swing set and a tree house, but no clothesline. The only way Goldie could have known that Patrick had superhero sheets was if she had slipped between them.

When confronted with the evidence, Goldie confessed and apologized. Patrick was so relieved that he read her a new story from *The Fairy Tales of the Brothers Grimm*.

Mrs. Behr took everyone out for ice cream to celebrate—everyone except Goldie. She was too busy sleeping—beautifully—while she waited for her prince to come.

Solution to *The Case of*
Shoeless Sam

The Sluggers didn't want Shoeless Sam to break the home run record, and they really didn't want the Gators to win the game. They had worked out a plan ahead of time to make sure that didn't happen.

As soon as Shoeless Sam left second base, two members of the Sluggers started a fistfight to block the crowd's view of third base. While the umpire and the crowd in the bleachers watched the fight, the player at third turned his base over. If Shoeless Sam's footprint wasn't on third, who could prove that he had actually touched the base?

It was the clean base that gave the Sluggers away. All of the other bases had muddy sneaker prints on them, along with Sam's footprint. Third base was clean, because no one had stepped on that side of the base.

Encyclopedia turned the base over again. Shoeless Sam's bare footprint was stamped right in the middle along with muddy sneaker prints. He was indeed the home run king.